Count The Aliens, Spaceships, Stars & Planets!

The perfect space counting book
for children aged 2-5

This book belongs to: _____

© PRINCE
JAMES PRESS

Welcome to Vol. 1!

*LEARNING THE KEY
SKILLS OF SEARCHING,
FINDING, OBSERVATION
AND COLOUR RECALL!*

Best of luck!

How many
green aliens
are there?

1   2   3   4   5

There are

 green aliens!

Are there **more planets** or **more spaceships?**

There are

4 **and** 2

planets **spaceships**

Which means that

there are more

planets than ***spaceships!***

How many blue rockets are there?

There are

3 blue rockets!

1   2   3

Count the
Planets!

There are four planets here...

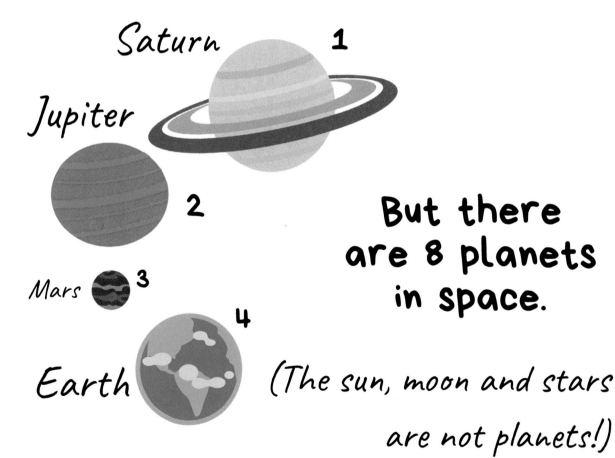

Saturn **1**

Jupiter **2**

Mars **3**

Earth **4**

But there are 8 planets in space.

(The sun, moon and stars are not planets!)

How many astronauts can you find?

There are

astronauts

1   2

Did you find the astronaut
in the top left corner?

How many
stars
can you count?

7 There are **stars!**

Did you find them all?

1 2 3 4 5 6 7

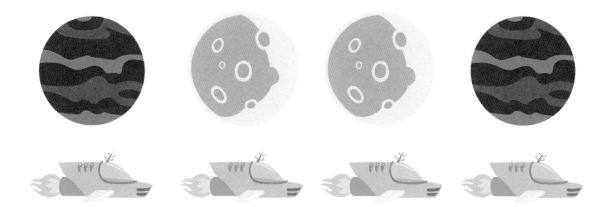

Count the
red planets!

There are **eight red planets!**

8

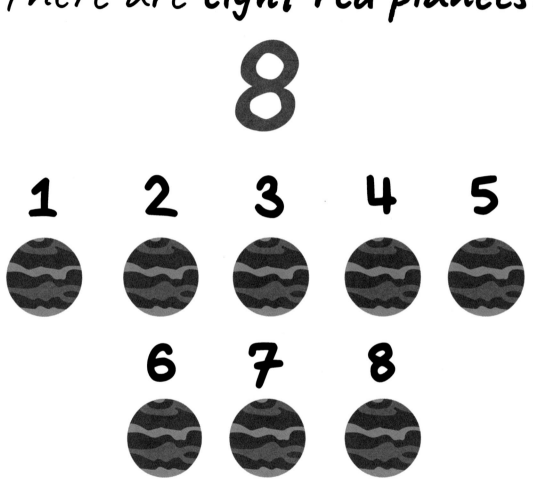

1   2   3   4   5

6   7   8

That's a lot of planets!

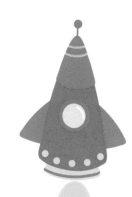

How many
moons
can you find?

There is only

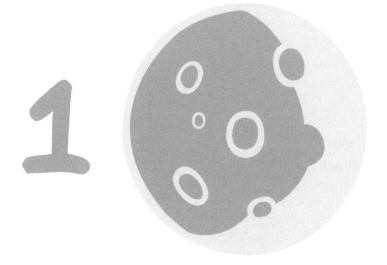

1 moon!

Can you see more aliens or more suns?

There are

10 and **5**

aliens   suns.

So there are more aliens

than suns!

Did you get it right? Get ready for the next counting question!

How many of the items fly in the sky?

All of the items fly in the sky!

1

2

3

4

5

6

How many planets have rings around them?

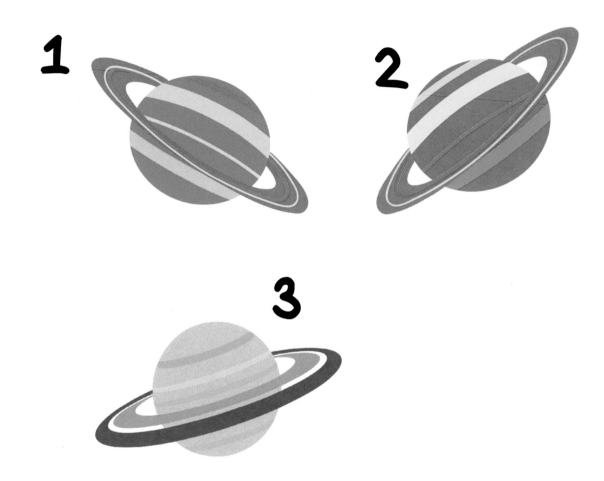

There are **three!**

In total, how many eyes?

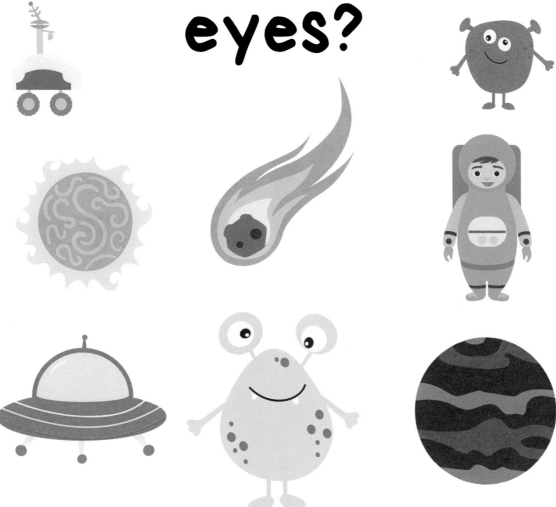

In total, there are
6 eyes!

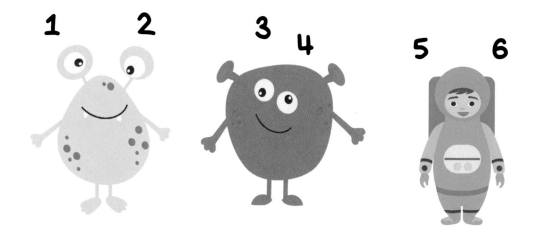

1 2   3 4   5 6

Did you count the two little eyes on the astronaut?

How many **blue** space supply ships are there?

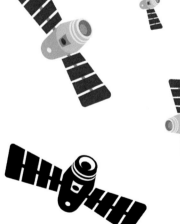

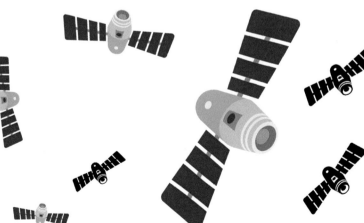

Nine

blue space supply ships!

Did you know - there are no astronauts working or living on space supply ships?

How many Letters?

I LOVE YOU TO THE MOON AND BACK

There are twenty-four letters in total!

That's a lot of numbers to count!
Did you get the right answer?

The last question!

Count the number
of times you see **planet earth**
in the whole book?

(including the one on this page, and including
those on answer pages!)

How many did
you count?
The answer is.....

Made in the USA
Monee, IL
08 October 2020